Calderdale

COMMUNITY

LIBRARIES, MUSEL

Books should be returned on or before the last date shown below. Any book **not required by another reader** may be renewed.

To renew, give your library membership number.

DATE DUE FOR RETURN		
2 9 JUL 2011		
1 0 AUG 2012		
my 8/13		
1 7 SEP 2014		
0 9 FEB 2015		
- 5 FEB 2016		

Prince Jasper the Unhelpful

S. J. Harris

Illustrated by Andy Catling

First published in Great Britain in 2010 by
TickTock Entertainment Ltd, The Old Sawmill,
103 Goods Station Road, Tunbridge Wells, Kent, TN1 2DP

ISBN: 978-1-84898-253-6 pbk

A CIP catalogue record for this book is available
from the British Library.

Printed in Great Britain by CPI Mackays, Chatham ME5 8TD

1 3 5 7 9 10 8 6 4 2

For my helpful princes,
Darren, James and Luke

Contents

Contents

Annoying the Servants

Prince Jasper loved giving useful advice. He didn't mean to interfere in other people's business but he simply couldn't stop himself. He was always full of good ideas and only ever wanted to be extremely helpful and to share his clever opinions with everybody around him. The trouble was that Prince Jasper's advice wasn't always that helpful. Sometimes it caused lots of problems and was extremely unhelpful.

Everybody in the palace liked

Prince Jasper, but they often wished he was helpful only some of the time. But Prince Jasper never, ever missed an opportunity to be extremely helpful all of the time.

All the servants had a story to tell about the time Prince Jasper had helped clean the palace. He'd polished the floors until they were as

slippery as ice rinks; rearranged the books in the library so well that his father couldn't find his favourite spy story; and re-hung the chandeliers, which promptly fell down again.

If Prince Jasper came across a servant happily mopping the palace floor, he couldn't just walk by and let them get on with it. Something like this would happen:

'You don't want to do it like that,' Prince Jasper would say, before snatching the mop from the bewildered servant. 'Let me show you how to do it. Five long strokes of the mop across the floor like so...'

SPLISH!

'And then repeat.'

SPLASH!

'You see? That's much better.'

SPLOSH!

The servant would smile through gritted teeth while Prince Jasper 'helpfully' sloshed dirty water across his nice shiny, clean floor.

'Thank you for being so very

helpful,' the servant would say grumpily. And as he started to mop the floor all over again, Prince Jasper would go in search of someone else to help.

It usually didn't take very long.

★ ★ ★

Yesterday, he had told Cook that his favourite cookies should each have exactly ten chocolate chips on top and ordered his maid to place his teddy bear right in the middle of the pillow in his four-poster bed. Then, after teaching his baby sister, Milly, the best way to blow raspberries in her milk, he decided to play outside. The Royal Butler and Bob the Boot Polisher dodged around the corner as he ran out through the front door.

'Phew! That was close!' Bob the Boot Polisher sighed with relief. 'Thank goodness Prince Jasper didn't see us. He has that look on his face.'

The Royal Butler frowned. 'You mean the I-know-a-better-way-to-do-that-than-you look?'

Bob nodded.

'I can't face being told how to polish my boots for the 100th time. Let's look for somewhere to hide until he's found somebody else to help today.'

The pair hurried away as Prince Jasper headed towards the orchards. Before long, he had bumped into Percy, the Royal Gardener, who was picking apples.

'Let me help you!' cried Prince Jasper.

Percy looked very worried. He

remembered the last time the prince had "helped" him. It had taken two years for his favourite apple tree to recover after Prince Jasper had given its branches a "small" trim.

Prince Jasper looked thoughtfully at the baskets of apples that Percy had spent hours collecting and he suddenly had a brilliant idea.

'You don't want to put the apples into lots of baskets. You should empty them into one big basket like this,' Prince Jasper said.

Before Percy could stop him, Prince Jasper picked up a basket, tripped and fell over. As he stood up, he slipped on an apple and knocked

over all the other baskets. Percy groaned as the apples rolled across the orchard.

'Thank you very much,' he sighed.

'Don't mention it.' Prince Jasper beamed. 'I like to help. That's why everybody calls me "Prince Jasper the Helpful".'

Percy began collecting the apples all over again. As soon as Prince Jasper was out of earshot he muttered something rude into the apple trees. Something that sounded remarkably like: 'Helpful? I really don't think so. I've never met anybody who meddles as much as him. "Prince Jasper the Unhelpful" is a far better name.'

Annoying the King

One bright summer morning, Prince Jasper was sitting at the breakfast table with his mother and father, King Monty and Queen Ella, while Milly slept in her cot. They were eating boiled eggs and soldiers, which just so happened to be the King's favourite. He hated runny yolks and liked them nice and firm. Prince Jasper didn't agree and when his father wasn't looking he helpfully pushed his runny egg in front of the King. Then he rolled his father's egg under the table.

'Here, try this!' Prince Jasper said,
giving his father's new egg a hard tap.

CRACK!

The egg split open and the golden
yolk poured over the King's plate.
Prince Jasper quickly dunked a
soldier into it.

'You see?' he beamed. 'It's much

better when the egg's runny.'

'How very helpful,' the King scowled. 'I'm glad you're around to tell me the best way to eat my eggs. I expect you'll be telling me how I should run my kingdom next?'

'Well, seeing that you're asking,' Prince Jasper began, 'a lot of people around here don't do very much. I'd throw them all into the dungeons. I know you work very hard, Father, but I'd have to send you there too.'

King Monty almost choked on his runny egg and his face turned bright red.

'Did I hear you right, dear?' Queen Ella frowned. 'Is your father taking a trip to the dungeons as well?'

'Yes, Mother,' said Prince Jasper.

'I think Father would find it helpful. He's always complaining that he doesn't have enough time to pick up a book. Dungeons are very quiet places so he'd get lots of reading done and he could get fit by running on the spot. It means he'd be able to keep up with me when we play football on Sundays and not get so out of breath.'

'Hurrumph. I'm extremely fit,' insisted the King, flexing his muscles.

'And what would you do after getting rid of your father, dear?' the Queen asked sweetly.

'I'd make every day a holiday, order everyone to eat chocolate cake for breakfast, lunch and dinner, and never make anyone wash behind their ears ever again,' Prince Jasper continued.

'Well, all that chocolate cake sounds good to me,' the Queen said enthusiastically. 'When can we start?'

'Enough!' the King snorted, banging his fist down hard on the table. 'I'm not going to the dungeons

and Cook already makes us ten chocolate cakes a week, Ella my dear. And as for you...'

The King glared at his son.

'Don't look like that, Father. In my opinion, that harsh frown doesn't suit you at all,' Prince Jasper said huffily. 'It makes you look at least five years older.'

'Does it now?' the King snapped. 'Well, *I* think we've had enough of your opinions for one breakfast time. Why don't you go outside and pester – I mean, help – someone else?'

'I'd love to,' Prince Jasper smiled. 'But I ran out of people to help before breakfast – I'm waiting for

Milly to wake up so I can tell her
the right way to crawl across the
floor without getting covered in dust.'

King Monty and Queen Ella
exchanged glances. The last time
Prince Jasper had "helped" Milly, he'd
taught her how to scream at the top
of her voice when she didn't get her
own way.

'I've got the feeling that Milly is going to be asleep for a very long time,' the Queen said slowly. 'I really don't think that you should wait for her. But maybe you could see if there's anyone outside the palace gates who needs your help. After all, you've helped so many people inside the palace.'

'Indeed,' the King chipped in. 'Perhaps there's someone in need of your advice. Someone who lives a long, long, long way away.'

'That's a brilliant idea,' Prince Jasper cried, clapping his hands together. 'There must be lots of people elsewhere who need my help in the kingdom.'

'I'm sure there are,' the King nodded encouragingly. 'You may even find a beautiful princess stuck in a tower somewhere who needs you to tell her how to escape.'

'Of course!' Prince Jasper exclaimed. 'As a matter of fact, I know the best way to rescue a princess from a tower. I was reading a book called *Escape Routes From Very Tall Towers* just last night.'

'It's settled then,' the Queen smiled. 'Off you go!'

'Never fear, princess!' Prince Jasper cried. 'I'm coming to rescue you.'

'Don't hurry back!' the King

shouted after him, as the prince
jumped on his horse Casper.
'Take as much time as you need.'

The Jewel "Polishers"

Prince Jasper was riding through the palace courtyard when he noticed a tall, thin man and a short, fat man who looked in need of his advice. They were trying to lift a chest of treasure on to the back of a horse in the stables. He guessed they must be the royal jewellers. He turned his horse around and trotted up to them.

'Good morning!' Prince Jasper said cheerily. 'Can I help you?'

The men jumped with surprise and the taller one accidentally let

go of the chest. It fell to the ground
CRASH! and landed on his friend's
foot.

'OW! Look what you're doing,
you clumsy idiot!' he cried, clutching
his big toe.

'That looks like a very heavy chest
of treasure,' Prince Jasper remarked. 'I
think it would be much better to use
a horse and cart. That way you

could carry all the treasure at once, instead of making several journeys.'

He nodded at the three chests on the ground that were crammed full of silver plates, gold spoons, diamond necklaces and three royal crowns.

'That sounds like very good advice,' the short, fat man said gruffly. 'We hadn't thought of that, had we, Sid?'

Sid sniggered.

'I like to help,' Prince Jasper said. 'You must be the jewellers who polish the Crown Jewels? Here, don't forget to take my crown as well. And remember, it should always be polished in a clockwise direction.'

24

He took his crown off his head
and passed it to Sid who was staring
at Prince Jasper in amazement.

Sid tossed the crown into one of
the chests. 'That's right, isn't it, Stan?
We're jewel thieves. Oops!
I mean jewel
polishers.'

'I thought
so.' Prince
Jasper said
with a nod.
'Look! There's
a cart over
there you can
use. Let me get it for you.'

Prince Jasper rushed to the cart

and brought it back. Then he helped the two men load the heavy chests onto it.

'I expect you're in a hurry, so it's best to use the gate over there,' he said, pointing across the courtyard. 'The guard always takes a nap at this time of day so you can go straight through without having to wake him.'

'Thanks for being so helpful, mate,' Stan chuckled. 'We won't forget you in a hurry, will we, Sid?'

'People do tend to remember me,' Prince Jasper admitted. 'Now I need to be off. I've got a beautiful princess to rescue.'

'Good luck!' Stan laughed. He pulled a scarf up to his eyes and drove the cart out of the courtyard at speed.

Prince Jasper was pleased he had already helped some strangers. He climbed back onto Casper and trotted past the snoozing guard.

A little further down the road, two soldiers on horseback caught up with him.

'Have you passed a couple of jewel thieves? They've escaped with the Crown Jewels!' one of the soldiers cried.

'No,' Prince Jasper said with a frown. 'But I'll keep my eyes open for the thieves.'

'Thanks,' the soldier replied. 'We'd best be going. There's no time to lose.'

'Absolutely,' said Prince Jasper. 'You should try and catch up with Sid and Stan – those nice men who polish the Crown Jewels. Maybe they've seen the thieves. I helped them load some chests of treasure onto a cart at the palace a little while ago.'

The soldiers rolled their eyes in exasperation and galloped away.

'They could have thanked me for my helpful advice,' Prince Jasper sniffed. 'Some people just don't have any manners!'

★ ★ ★

For the rest of the morning, Prince
Jasper searched high and low for a
princess who was in desperate need
of his help. He was disappointed –
apart from the ungrateful soldiers, he
hadn't been able to help anyone else
along the way. The cows in the field

had rolled their eyes, turned their backs and refused to follow his advice about the best way to chew grass. A blackbird had even aimed a dropping at his head when he suggested it changed its tune. Luckily, Prince Jasper had managed to duck at the last minute and the mess landed SPLAT! by his left foot.

At last, Prince Jasper spotted a very tall golden tower in the distance. He peered through his telescope. Yes, there was a beautiful, red-haired princess sitting at a high window,

hammering away at a typewriter. He remembered a very useful chapter in the book he'd been reading, *Escape Routes From Very Tall Towers*. It was time to put Plan A into action.

'Don't worry, beautiful princess. I'm here to rescue you!' Prince Jasper shouted.

The princess saw a little figure galloping towards her and tutted loudly.

'Not another stupid prince,' she snarled. 'Why can't they leave me alone to write my book?'

She quickly typed out a note, ran down the stairs and pinned it onto the front door of the tower.

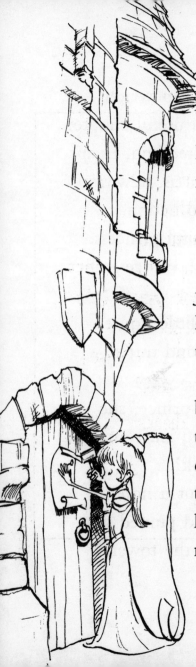

'I hope he knows how to read,' she muttered and settled down to her writing again.

Prince Jasper jumped down from his horse and spotted the note.

'Aha. A letter begging me to help this poor damsel in distress,' he smiled. But the grin was wiped off his face as he began reading. The note said:

Dear Prince,
I don't want to be rescued.
Clear off before I throw
a bucket of water over you.
I just want some peace and quiet
while I write my book: **What It's
Really Like To Be a Beautiful
Princess: Warts and All**. Please
go away and leave me alone.

Yours Without Any Thanks
Whatsoever,
Princess Miranda

'The poor princess!' Prince Jasper exclaimed loudly. 'She must have gone a little mad after being stuck in her tower for so long. Everyone knows that a beautiful princess needs a strong, handsome prince.'

'Excuse me!' Princess Miranda shouted. She was leaning out of the window with a megaphone pressed to her lips.

'Which part of my note didn't you understand?' she boomed. 'I'm quite happy in my tower and I don't need rescuing. And I'm fed up with stupid princes dashing over here and trying to kick my front door in. It's costing me a fortune

in new locks.'

'In my opinion…' Prince Jasper
shouted.

'I'm not interested in your
opinion,' Princess Miranda scowled.

'But…'

'Well, don't say I didn't warn you.'

Princess Miranda bent over and
picked up one of the many buckets
of water she kept handy to throw
over unwanted princes. She promptly
poured it over Prince Jasper's head.

SPLASH! SPLOOSH!

'AAAAAAGGGGGGHHHHHH!'
he shouted.

Prince Jasper backed off to a safe
distance, out of reach of Princess

Miranda's buckets of water. He was cold and wet but wasn't discouraged. He was right and this extremely rude princess was wrong.

She needed to be rescued. She just didn't know it yet!

It was time for Plan B.

The Ungrateful
Princess

Prince Jasper unrolled the rope ladder
from his backpack. It had two hooks
at one end and was long enough to
reach to the very top of the tower.
He just needed to throw it through
the window and hook the ladder
onto something solid. Unfortunately
for him, it hooked over Princess
Miranda's foot and she wasn't very
impressed.

'Are you still here?' she snarled.
She unhooked the ladder and

waited for a couple
of minutes. When
Prince Jasper was
halfway up, she
tossed the ladder
out of the window.

'AAAAAGGGG
GGGGHHHHH!'
the prince cried,
as he plunged
to the ground.

THUD!

'That should do
it.' Princess Miranda
muttered.

Prince Jasper
was battered and

bruised, but he wasn't put off.

It was time for Plan C.

The tightrope.

Prince Jasper climbed to the top of a tall tree opposite the tower while Princess Miranda watched very closely.

'It's only fair to warn you that I wouldn't do whatever you're about to do,' she threatened. 'It will only end in tears.'

'I promise not to make you cry,' Prince Jasper replied. 'But you're coming down from that tower.'

'Is that so?' Princess Miranda bellowed through her megaphone.

Prince Jasper nodded.

He fastened a piece of strong string
to the highest branch of the tree.
Then he tied a stone to
the other end and threw
it through the tower
window. There was a loud
crash as the stone smashed
into Princess Miranda's
favourite china duck and landed
on the floor.

'You interfering little busybody!'
she shouted. 'Look what you've done.'

'You'll thank me when you're out
of the tower,' Prince Jasper insisted.

He stepped onto the tightrope,
which swung to the left and then to
the right while he stood very still and

tried to get his balance. Prince Jasper
wibbled and wobbled and wibbled
and wobbled some more. He began
walking carefully towards the tower
as Princess Miranda appeared at the
window again, brandishing a pair of
sharp scissors. She had a very sour
look on her face, as if she'd just
sucked a particularly sharp lemon.

'Perhaps you're right,' she said

sweetly. 'Maybe I do need to listen
to your advice.'

'Excellent!' Prince Jasper said
through gritted teeth.

He was concentrating hard as
he balanced on the tightrope and
didn't look at the princess.

'Do you know the best way to
cut a piece of string?' Princess
Miranda asked.

'Oh, that's simple,' Prince Jasper replied airily. 'You just need a pair of very sharp scissors. Then make one good firm cut.'

'Really? Like this?' Princess Miranda asked.

SNIP!

She cut the tightrope in two and

WHOOSH! Prince Jasper plunged to the ground.

CRASH! BANG! OUCH!

For the first time in his life, Prince Jasper wished he hadn't tried to be so helpful.

'Are you still alive?' Princess Miranda shouted.

'I think so,' Prince Jasper said weakly, rubbing his head. 'Just.'

'Dash!' Princess Miranda muttered. 'Better luck next time. Are you going home now?'

'No,' he said, staggering to his feet.

Princess Miranda thought for a moment and looked hard at Prince Jasper. 'That's good,' she said slyly, 'because I've changed my mind. I think I do really need your help to get out of this tower after all.'

'Of course! How can I be of service, beautiful princess?' Prince Jasper cried with delight.

He beamed brightly at Princess Miranda, who had an odd little smile on her face. He was thrilled that she was finally prepared to listen to his very helpful advice.

The Princess and
the Catapult

'I want to know the best way to build a giant catapult,' Princess Miranda shouted through her megaphone. 'Do you have any suggestions?'

Prince Jasper frowned. He thought that being catapulted through the air

was an odd way
to escape from a
tower, but he was
so pleased the
princess wanted
his help that he
didn't argue.

'Luckily for
you, I know exactly
how to build a giant
catapult. I was reading all about
it just the other day.'

'Well?' Princess Miranda asked,
raising an eyebrow.

'You'll need lots of giant elastic
bands and a couple of large planks
of wood.'

'Great, thanks. Now, what sort of ammunition should I use?'

'Why do you need ammunition if we're going to fire *you* from the catapult?' Prince Jasper asked, looking puzzled.

'I just want to make sure that it's working before I sit in it,' Princess Miranda smirked. 'I was thinking about using something from the kitchen, but it's probably not a good idea to waste fresh fruit and vegetables in the catapult. What do you think?'

'I agree. You should only use really old, stinky food that you've thrown away. How about some rotten eggs?

You must have some of those in your rubbish bin.'

'Excellent,' Princess Miranda smiled, as she scribbled notes. 'Is there anything else I should look for?'

'I'd recommend some nice rotten

cabbage, old sardines,
some very ripe bananas
and perhaps a smelly
piece of cheese
or two.'

'Brilliant!' Princess Miranda
beamed. 'I'd never have
thought of all that.'

Prince Jasper smiled. Princess
Miranda had finally seen sense.
He'd have her out of her tower in
no time. Then he could give her lots
more advice, especially about the
best place to live. She'd be much
happier in a nice cottage by the sea
rather than in a draughty tower in
the middle of nowhere. He could

also show her how to make the world's best peanut butter sandwich and teach her how to tie her hair into pigtails.

'Right!' announced Princess Miranda. 'Now, can you tell me how to build the catapult?'

'Of course!'

Things were getting better and better. It suddenly dawned on Prince Jasper that she was the first person who had actually asked him for help. The thousands of other times, he'd simply given away his advice for free. He felt very pleased with himself as he gave the princess very detailed instructions about how to build the catapult and fire it.

'Fantastic! I'm just about done.'
Princess Miranda grinned. 'Do I need
anything else?'

'Well, you need someone to help
you fire the catapult. It will be much
quicker if two of you keep loading
the rotten food. Then your helper
can fire you from the catapult
when you've finished testing it.'

'Brilliant!' Princess Miranda
exclaimed. 'Nurse? Can you come
here for a second?'

An elderly woman joined Princess
Miranda at the window. Prince Jasper
didn't like the way she grinned
nastily at him. He gulped and took

a step back as he noticed the rotten, stinky food spilling over the sides of the catapult.

'Well, I think we're just about ready,' Princess Miranda smirked. 'Finally, what advice would you give someone who was just about to be pelted with rotten fruit and vegetables?'

Prince Jasper
turned
white as
he finally
realized
what
Princess
Miranda had
been up to all along.

'They should run like the wind,'
he squealed.

He turned on his heels, but he
wasn't quick enough. Princess
Miranda started firing her giant
catapult which, thanks to his helpful
advice, was amazingly efficient.

A rotten egg landed on Prince Jasper's head.

SPLAT!

Then a rotten cabbage.

SPLIDGE!

Then a stinky piece of cheese and a sardine.

SQUELCH!

Prince Jasper jumped on his horse and galloped away as fast as he could, but the smelly food just kept on flying. Nurse continued to load the machine, while Princess Miranda

fired and fired until her fingers were red and sore.

As he fled, Prince Jasper wished he hadn't tried to be so helpful.

Enough Help for One Day

By the time Princess Miranda's catapult had run out of ammunition, Prince Jasper was covered from head to toe in disgusting gunk. PHE-EW! He smelt extremely bad. The pong was so awful that several birds fainted and fell out of their nests as he rode by.

Prince Jasper was very upset and wasn't his usual self at all. Instead of being neat and tidy, he looked as if he'd dived head first into a dustbin.

When he passed a shepherd tending
his flock, he wasn't tempted to tell
him the best way to hold his crook.
Instead, he stayed completely silent.
The shepherd, however, had
something he wanted to say:

'If you want my advice, you
should have a bath and wash your

clothes, young man. You stink!'

'If I wanted your advice, I'd ask for it,' Prince Jasper muttered darkly.

But, whether he liked it or not, he was given lots of helpful advice by people he passed. Things like:

'If I were you, I wouldn't wear a cabbage behind my ear.'

'I'm not sure smelly cheese and sardines make a good shampoo.'

'Who told you rotten eggs are good for your skin? They were lying.'

'In my opinion, it's better to eat food than wear it.'

Prince Jasper was sick and tired of people giving him advice by the time he arrived home. He stormed into the palace without telling the servants how to open the front door, and raced up to his room.

Once inside, Prince Jasper tore off his clothes and jumped into a steaming hot bath with his yellow plastic duck. His servant was pleasantly surprised to discover that, for the first time ever, he didn't tell him the correct temperature of bath water.

'It's been a horrible day,' Prince Jasper confided in his duck. 'But I'm

beginning to feel a little better now.
Thank you for asking.'

Next, Prince Jasper went to find
Milly, who was being given her
bath by her nanny. He helped wash
her and didn't tell her the best way

to kick her legs in the water to make a really big splash. Instead, Prince Jasper kept his opinions to himself.

A little while later, Prince Jasper was sitting at the dinner table with his mother and father. He was feeling much better.

'Did you have a good day, dear?' Queen Ella asked, adjusting the paper crown that was slipping off her head. 'We weren't expecting you back so soon.'

'Yes, are you *sure* there aren't more people out there who need your advice?' King Monty chipped in, tugging at his lopsided paper crown.

'Our soldiers are still looking for those "jewellery polishers" you ran into today.'

Prince Jasper blushed.

'Maybe you could suggest how your mother and I can get our crowns back?' his father continued. 'Cook found these old party hats in the attic, but they keep falling off. We want our gold crowns back. They're much easier to keep on our heads.'

Prince Jasper shook his head slowly.

'I'd love to help catch Stan and Sid, really I would, but I think I've given enough advice for one day.'

His parents almost fell off their chairs with surprise.

'Really?' the King gasped. 'Are you sure you don't want to tell me the best way to carve this juicy joint of beef? Shouldn't the slices of meat be paper thin? I seem to remember you telling me that interesting fact last Sunday.' The King and Queen both held their breath as Prince Jasper hesitated.

'I don't have any useful advice,' he admitted finally. 'I'm sure the beef will be wonderful, however you decide to carve it.'

'Excellent news!' the King exclaimed, banging his fist on the table with delight. 'I'm glad to hear it. But I've noticed that you're a little

70

different tonight, son. Are you feeling quite well?'

'Yes, Father,' Prince Jasper said. 'It's just that I've decided that I'm never going to interfere in anyone's business ever again!'

The King tried to hide a smile.

'I've been trying to be helpful all day and it hasn't worked,' Prince Jasper continued. 'From now on, I'm not going to help unless someone asks me first.'

'That's very wise, dear,' the Queen smiled. 'Why don't you eat up before your dinner gets cold?'

Prince Jasper managed to get through the meal without criticizing the way his mother dished up the vegetables. He even stayed silent when a servant poured custard over his jam pudding and accidentally splashed the tablecloth.

'If you don't mind, I'd like to go to bed now,' Prince Jasper said,

yawning. 'All that not helping has tired me out!'

'An early night? Even better!' The King beamed. 'I mean, whatever you think is best, son.'

'Yes. You need to get your rest before another tiring day of not helping tomorrow,' agreed the Queen.

Prince Jasper nodded. He kissed his parents goodnight and climbed the long staircase to his bedroom. He didn't move his teddy bear closer to the middle of his pillow, adjust the rug even a little bit or twitch his curtains. He simply climbed into his pyjamas, jumped into bed and pulled the covers over him.

Just as Prince Jasper was about to close his eyes, he spotted a mouse scurrying across the floor with a piece of cheese in its mouth. He sat bolt upright in bed.

'I don't like to interfere because I definitely don't do that sort of thing any more,' he bellowed. 'But if you did ask for my advice, I'd tell you to balance the cheese on your nose. That way you won't be tempted to eat it before you get home.'

The mouse jumped with fright,
dropped the cheese and scuttled away.

'But you didn't ask for my advice,
so I'm not going to say a word,'
Prince Jasper yawned.

He lay back in bed, pleased that
he hadn't been tempted
to interfere.

Just then his
mother popped
her head around
the door to say
goodnight.

'I thought I
heard a noise. Is
everything all right
in here?' she asked.

'Yes, thank you, Mother. I'm being very quiet. It was the mouse who was being noisy.'

'A mouse?' she cried, spinning around. 'Where?'

'Don't worry, Mother. I know you're scared of mice, so I shooed him away.'

'I'm glad to hear it, Jasper. I'll leave the door open a little so you can still see the light from the landing.'

Prince Jasper watched as she slowly closed the door.

'How's that?' she asked.

'Can you close the door just a little bit more please. There's too much light.'

'And now?'

'There's not enough light. The gap
in the door should be just as wide as

your thumb, you know,' he said sleepily.

'Silly me,' his mother laughed. 'How could I forget? Goodnight, Jasper.'

'Goodnight.'

Prince Jasper yawned, rolled over and thought sleepily about all the people he wouldn't help in the morning.

'Top of the list are those cheeky jewel thieves,' he muttered to himself. No, he definitely wouldn't give Stan and Sid any useful advice if he ever bumped into them again...

The Unhelpful Prince and the Jewel Thieves

Look out for the next title
in Autumn 2010!

Author Biography

Sarah grew up in Sutton Coldfield, West Midlands and gained a 2.1 degree in English Literature from Nottingham University. She trained as a journalist at the *Western Daily Press* in Bristol and has worked for the *Daily Mail* since 1999 as a general reporter, Midlands correspondent and education correspondent.

Sarah now has a weekly education column in the *Daily Mail*. She lives in West London with her husband and two young sons.